Alvin can't Jump

Jacquelyn Hester Colleton-Akins
and Elbert Akins III

ReadersMagnet, LLC

DEDICATION

To my children, to my
grandchildren, my cousins,
my niece, and my siblings. In
addition, to all men and women
who are servers to the most
high in the Heavenly father I
am that I am and his son.

On a warm sunny morning in the month of Av July-August. The dawning of a new day was imminent in a large pond, located in the countryside adjacent to Float Water Park. The name of this large pond is called Maybank Pond. In this fascinating location, you will find all different kinds of lively animals and people gathering around Maybank Pond.

The primarily reason why people and animals come to Maybank Park and Pond is for recreation during the different seasons whether it be Fall, Winter, Spring, or Summer.

During the changing of the different seasons at Maybank Pond the animals and people enjoy the fresh clean water and smell the clean air. People will enjoy the beautiful flowers, and mother nature. Animals can be seen in the distance watching from afar. The different changes and levels of the ecosystem can be seen in the trees, plants, and female animals giving birth to young animals.

Maybank Pond is the ideal place for relaxation and to have lots of fun for picnics for example family gatherings, BBQ, playing games, boat rides, playing sports, playing with pets, children playing, going on nature walks, and just enjoying the scenery.

In Maybank pond you will find different kinds of animals such as:

Deer

Squirrel

Racoon

Beaver

2

Bird

Deer

Snake

Lizard

Turtle

Frog

Horse

Fox

Hummingbird

Honey bee (In
beehive in a tree)

In Maybank pond you will find different flowers such as:

Rose

Lily pad

Petunia

Violet

Orchid

Sunflower

The flowers grows very beautifully wild like everywhere all over the park. The park cleaning crew keeps the park neat and beautiful for everyone to enjoy.

In Maybank park you will find different types of trees such as:

Oak Tree

Walnut

Sequoia tree

Magnolia tree

Maple tree

Each tree is kept in line very neatly and very colorful with the seasons.

In Maybank pond you will find different plants such as:

Fern   Daffodil

Dandelion

Each plant is kept in line very neatly and very colorful with the seasons.

In Maybank Pond and Float Water Park you will find the appealing ecosystem meeting site will always be an educational and breathtaking place for animals and people to visit.

Here, in Maybank Pond is the most lively animal kingdom, you can see the baby animals playing, swimming, and interacting with each other. The ducks are feasting on pond weeds, grass, seeds, eggs, and snails.

As time progressed don't fail to take note that some female frogs beginning to appear restless. This type of behavior comes about, due to the fact that these special frogs are expecting to give birth to new tadpoles.

A tadpole is a stage in the life cycle of amphibians like frogs. The tadpole is a larval stage, or a period in the cycle of some animals where the offsprings look nothing like the adult. A tadpole lives almost entirely in the water, although there are some amphibian species where the tadpole a can survive on land.

The tadpole must undergo a series of physical changes called metamorphosis before it becomes an adult.

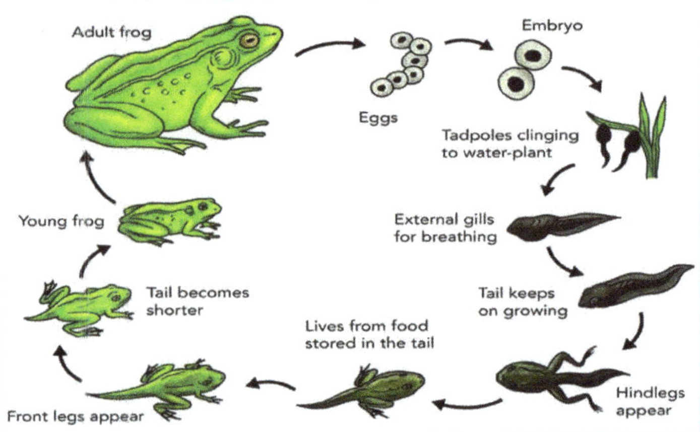

THE TADPOLE STAGES

Stage 1: Eggs

The eggs are laid in a gelatinous mass, and eventually as the eggs develop you can see a tiny tadpole - like critters inside of the egg. Of course it depends on the species, but most eggs hatch after about 6 to 21 days.

Stage 2: Hatching between 6 to 21 days

Soon after hatching, the tadpoles are most at risk of being eaten. To avoid the predators or being apart of the food chain, they affix themselves to weeds and try to blend in with their environment. No need to swim around looking for food, they get their nutrients from remnants that is already in their belly.

Stage 3: Free Swimming 7 to 10 weeks

The tadpoles will release itself from the weeds and begin to swim. At this stage, the tadpole will eat algae or other tiny plant matter

Stage 4: Teeth development

During this stage of development the teeth is very important because development takes place within the teeth around the 4 weeks. The tadpole's diet can diversify to include more plants and possibly small insects. This is mainly due to the development of teeth, as well as the guts of the animal becoming more complex. Skin slowly starts to cover the gills as the tadpole will utilize lungs instead of gills by the time it becomes an adult and to be able to croak.

Stage 5: Legs

During these weeks of 5 to 9, the tadpole begins to sprout legs and its body starts to look more frog-like and less tadpole-like. The tadpole may begin to consume massive insects.

Stage 6: Froglet

During the 12th week, the tadpole is called a froglet, looks like a frog with a tail. For the first time the froglet can finally leave the water "leaping, splashing and gazing at everything insight and making vocal sounds like "croaking, croaking, croaking".

"MY NAME IS ALVIN" and this is my story. You might say, I am the blessed one. After my birth, I experienced all kinds of physical and emotional problems. Needless to say, "I still imagined myself having hope to overcome the odds against me". Please allow me to begin by saying, my mother, a female frog, gave birth to four thousand eggs at a time. Which are fertilized by the male frog. Frogs become sexually mature approximately four years of age. They emerge from hibernation during the months Adar February to March to seek out breeding grounds. The female frogs lays her eggs in shallow water. It takes about 40 days for tadpoles to emerge from their eggs. When the eggs are mature, the male frog position itself on the female back and wrap his forelimbs around her middle section in amplexus or pseudocopulation, which can last several days. Under pressure from am plexus, the female frog releases mature eggs through cloaca located near the hind legs. The male frog immediately releases seminal fluid from the male cloaca, pouring it over the eggs as they are released from the female. The eggs are immediately fertilized before dropping them into the water. When a female is within ten days of fertilization, the embryo develops into a tadpole and emerges from the egg with strong wiggly movements. Young tadpoles feed on microscopic plants beneath the surface of the water. After two months the tadpoles develops lungs and pokes their heads above the water surface, using newly developed lungs to gulp air. The tadpole's hind legs and tail are fully developed at this stage.

On a beautiful Summer day, months later mother frog gave birth to four thousand eggs. All of the eggs were born healthy except one. "This is where the story gets interesting", following after those forty days the tadpoles emerges from being eggs to tadpoles. When Mother frog saw that I was unable to swim, she quickly approached me and gazed at me with a mean look on her face. Then, she took her right hind leg and kicked me to the other side of Maybank Pond wall, the kick was so severe I was unconscious for three days. When I became conscious no one was by my side, to rescue me or take care of me. I weeped and was hungry and thirsty for nutrients and my body was hurting due to hitting the wall. My body was in pain but

I had pushed myself to move. Weeks have passed and I never saw my family ever again.

"Two months of my life went by so strangely", not one frog or tadpole came over to my home to check on me or to see if I needed anything. One day, I even called out to a group of tadpoles that was swimming close by and I ask them to me "help me, I am sick, please help me", they kept swimming right on by. I realized from that moment on I was alone in this pond called Maybank Pond. I climbed up with my forearms and looked into the sky and said, "Heavenly Father help me endure my handicapped life, without hind legs and build my confidence to endure what I have to go through to achieve my goals in life. No one here to help me but you Heavenly Father and your son, Vish-she-ya.

Today is a new day and I will select this left side of Maybank Pond and two beautiful lily pads, perennials, algae, a rock, violets and ferns to be my new home. I received my name Alvin from the from the Heavenly Father. I love my name Alvin because of its meaning which is wise. I will register myself for school and get an education. I feel good about today and my new beginnings. I am different because I was born with a disability, no hind legs and the world sees me as a outcast. I will function without hind legs because I see myself as a whole person. I love life.

It has been seven years living at Maybank Pond, I completed school and I feel good about myself. Let me have a reflection on what I went through. I chose not to take part in my high school graduation. I made A's on my report card and I was a obedient student in all of my classes. My reflection will be my graduation of walking down the line of accomplishment and hardship I went through because I won and accomplished my goals in life. I had no one to love me, no one to talk or play with. No classmates at school would ask me to play with them. On a daily basis, I received rejections from my peers, ate lunch by myself in the cafeteria. My teacher never said anything to me nor even call on me in class. On a positive note though, "I found joy playing by myself and at times played with the magnificent butterflies, birds, and other insects". The best part about my education, I received my high school diploma and now I am off to college.

I have finished a milestone and now I'm ready to embark on a new journey to college. "Night-time is approaching and I must make it across the bottom of the lake to make it home safe. One of the hardest thing to deal with, is I am alone and I have no one to share my success story with. Each night I would position myself in my corner in the lake on my special lily pad and look steadily up at the sky staring directly at the bright moon and stars." Then I would think to myself, "how splendid the moon is in its own glory". Then I would thank the Creator for having the moon to provide light for the night. During the day I would thank the Creator for having the sun to shine with cheerful brightness, warmness, and coziness. Apologized for treating Alvin bad for not calling him.- Then I would thank the Creator for the clouds being so fluffy and breathtaking. To the Creator be all the glory! He has been supplying all my needs and caring for me since

I've been an orphan. This is my prayer, "Dear Heavenly Father with your help, I managed to get through a long day without any contact or collaboration with my peers. My petition is for you to continue helping me and to forgive my family and peers for hurting me. "Please give me the strength to release the bitterness and humiliation I have harbored in my heart". "You have taught me to speak affirmations over my circumstances and situations". I am healed, I am whole and worthy to be loved in Yish-she-ya's name. Please provide me with an amicable relationship with someone special at Maybank Pond. In conclusion, I ask you to keep everyone safe in the pond and around the pond. Give everyone a good night sleep and bless me with two hind legs to jump and leap for you". Shalom!

This is a new day, I am starting college and I am very excited and hoping that I will be able to meet a friend. I have to journey a little further this morning to travel for college. I started pulling myself down to the bottom of the pond then I heard someone shouting "Good morning, good morning, good morning". I was a little startled and asked, "Are you talking to me?" and the frog replied, "Yes, I am talking to you, what are you doing at the bottom of Maybank pond'? "Come down and see", Alvin replied. "What is your name?" Alvin asked. "My name is Dottie, What is your name?" Dottie asked. "My name is Alvin," Alvin said with a big smile. Dottie, let me explain to you, the reason why I am at the bottom of the pond is, "by any chance, have you notice that I do not have hind legs?" Oh Alvin, I am so sorry! What happened? Let's discuss this at a later time so we won't be late for class". Alvin and Dottie begin a friendship as they strolling together and talking with a smile on their faces to class. After class Alvin and Dottie strolled to the bottom of the pond.

For the first time Alvin had someone to communicate with. He had a big smile on his face. Alvin asked Dottie what was her major? and she replied, "Political Science, I would like to be the first female frog President in 2020. I want to be a President to build bridges and tear down walls that take violence away from happening and striving for peace and love for everyone. What is your major Alvin? "My major is Biology, I want to be a Pediatrician to treat all children tadpoles and frogs of all kinds."

Dottie? Do you have anyone special in your life? She replied no ... Alvin, how about you? Lovely Dottie, absolutely no one in my life. Will we see each other again? Of course by all means. Good bye ... don't forget to complete your homework.

For the rest of the week, Dottie and Alvin made their way to Maybank pond college campus. Alvin was so delighted to have someone to talk to after class and going back home. Dottie told Alvin goodbye and Alvin told Dottie we will see each other in the morning, "sweet dreams". Alvin laid down on his lily pad and prayed asking the Heavenly Father for his hind legs and to thank him for meeting Dottie, his first and only friend. Thank you Heavenly Father, it was so wonderful having someone to talk to and be with in Maybank Pond.

Early the next morning Alvin woke up feeling wonderful about himself and thinking about his only new lady friend he met. Alvin did not pay any attention to himself by doing his normal morning routine and pulled himself down to the bottom of the pond.

Alvin dragging his himself down to the bottom of the pond not realizing he has two hind legs. Later, Dottie met Alvin at the pond and she looked down at Alvin's body and saw his two hind legs. Dottie immediately shouted, "Alvin, Alvin! you have two hind legs, you have two hind legs!". Alvin responded, "Yeah, yeah, come on down Dottie so we can get to class because we are late". Dottie yelled, "Stop Alvin and look at your legs". Alvin stopped and looked and touched his hind legs. Alvin shouted, "I have legs, I have legs". Dottie shouted, "Yes Alvin! you have legs the Heavenly Father have blessed you with legs". Dottie instructed Alvin to jump to her.

Alvin was so elated " he yelled! **Wheeee! Yippee! He yelled"** Wha·a·a·a t? I got legs! to be a normal frog because he looked, walked, leaped, and jumped like a froggy. He was able to parade his lady friend with proudness and confidence. All the other frogs (froggies) and animals had their eyes on Alvin and Dottie.

Alvin went to the restroom to take time for himself and to reflect on how amazing the Heavenly Father has been to him and blessed him with his two hind legs. There is nothing too difficult for the Creator.

Alvin's classmates came up to him and congratulated him for his hind legs and they apologized for treating him so bad. Apologized for treating Alvin bad for not calling him.

The Dean over the university walked up to Alvin and congratulated him for his hind legs and being a excellent role model. The Dean apologized for treating Alvin unfair. Dottie encouraged to Alvin cheer up! "Your faith has healed you, "Your Heavenly Father has done marvelous things in your life. I see that you are loved, gifted and strong".

At three o'clock after class, Dottie had a surprise for me. We traveled to the west end of Maybank College. This was where all the students met after class for relaxation and fun after an interesting day of class. For example, boat riding, surfing, scuba diving, bungee jumping, swimming, lounging, picnics, socializing, romancing, tunnel of love, high frogjurnplng, and doing homework. This was Alvin's first time ever meeting at this cozy location, because he had no friends in the past, he never visited this enchanted area. Being at this specific place for a pleasant outing. Alvin was very ecstatic to visit Float Water Park.

After leaving Float Water Park, Alvin and Dottie headed back to Maybank Pond filled with thrills and excitement. This sensational couple was hopping together, leaping together, making frog noises, diving into the pond and splashing water everywhere. "Love was in the air". Needless to say, Alvin was receiving the answer to a portion of his prayer from the Creator. No doubt he was basking in the sun and enjoying an amicable relationship with his future wife. Then, Alvin popped the question to Dottie, "Would you like to be my wife?". Dottie responded by saying, "Yes! of course, I would love to be your wife". Alvin having the look of joy and a big smile on his face. At this romantic spot Alvin was so close to Dottie and he didn't care who was watching. He presented Dottie with an engagement ring and one beautiful yellow rose. Dottie exhibited a big beautiful smile and tears rolled down her cheeks and she accepted the ring and the rose. Dottie stated to Alvin, "I love you", and Alvin stated, "I love you too" Dottie. The two of them shared a kiss of love.

The couple has been married for eleven months. Alvin and Dottie are expecting their first four thousand tadpoles. Alvin and Dottie promised they will love all of their babies unconditionally, no matter how their born and what they look like. They will take care of them with the best of their ability and love them all equally. They are a family and will stay together as a family until they are grown and start their own family.

The End

GLOSSARY

1. Adaptation - Special way that a plant lives.

2. Adjacent - Next to something else.

3. Algae - Plants that do not have tubes. Algae lives in the oceans, lakes, and ponds.

4. Bark - Tough outside layer of a tree trunk.

5. Biology - Study of living organisms.

6. Botany - Study of plants.

7. Breeding - Mating and production of offspring by animals.

8. Bulb - Underground stem with leaves that store food.

9. Carbon dioxide - Gas from the air.

10. Cells - Tiny parts that plants are made up of.

11. Chlorophyll - material that makes leaves green.

12. Cloaca - Common cavity at the end of the digestive tract.

13. Conservation - Protection and wise use of natural resources.

14. Deciduous - A tree that loses all its leaves at a certain time each year. Oak and maple trees are deciduous.

15. Deciduous forest - Forest that is made up of deciduous trees.

16. Development - Process of developing.

17. Disability - Physical and mental condition that limits a person's movements, senses, and activities.

18. Ecosystem - A biological community of interacting organisms.

19. Egg - Round object laid by a female bird, reptile, and fish.

20. Embryo - A unborn offspring in the process of development.

21. Environment - Place where plants and animals live.

22. Evergreen -Tree that does no lose all its leaves in the fall.

23. Fascinating - Captivate

24. Female - Sex that can bear offspring or produce eggs.

25. Ferns - Plants with roots.

26. Fertilization - The action or process of fertilizing an egg.

27. Fertilized - To develop a new individual by introducing male reproductive material.

28. Forest - Place where many trees grow. Smaller plants and variety of animals are also found in the forest.

29. Forelimbs - Either of the front limbs of an animal.

30. Free swimming - Able to swim freely.

31. Froglet - A tiny frog.

32. Handicapped - Condition that restricts one's ability to function physically, mentally, and socially.

33. Hatching- To come forth from the egg.

34. Heavenly father - I am that I am.

35. Hibernation - Condition or period of an animal or plant spending the winter sleeping.

36. Imminent - About to happen.

37. Leaves - Parts of a plant where food is made.

38. Metamorphosis - Change of the form or nature.

39. Microscopic plants - tiny life forms organisms, often consisting of a single cell, and very sensitive to change.

40. Mold - Kind of a fungi.

41. Moss - Small plant that does not have tubes.

42. Natural resources- Things on Earth people find useful. Water is natural resource.

43.   Nectar - Sweet liquid made inside a flower.

44.   Nutrients - Substance that provides nourishments essential for growth.

45.   Ovary - Part of a flower that hold the egg cells.

46.   Oxygen - Leaves of plants give off.

47.   Pediatrician - A Child's doctor.

48.   Perennial - Plant that grows year after year without being replanted.

49.   Petals - Parts of flowers that are usually colored.

50.   Photosynthesis - Plants make food.

51.   Pistil - Female part of a flower.

52.   Plants - Grow, produce, and make their own food. Plants have roots, stems, and leaves.

53.   Political science - Branch of knowledge that deals with systems of government.

54.   Pollen - Yellow powder made by the male parts of the flower.

55. Pollination - Moving pollen from the stamens of a flower to the pistil.

56. President - Elected head of republican state. Ex: President Barack Obama and President John F. Kennedy.

57. Reproduce - Make more living things.

58. Root- Part of plant that is in the ground.

59. Root hair - Tips of roots are covered with tiny root hairs that take in water from the soil.

60. Pseudocopulation - Attempted copulation by a male insect with a flower that resembles a flower.

61. Seed - Part of plant that can grow into a new plant.

62. Seminal fluid - Part of semen that is produce by many accessory glands such as prostate gland and seminal vesicles.

63. Sepals - Parts of a flower that protect the flower when it is a bud. Sepals look like leaves.

64. Sexually - relates to the two sexes or to a gender.

65. Shalom - Hebrew for closing out a prayer.

66. Spore - Special cell that can live a long time without water.

67. Stage - Period in a process.

68. Stamens - Male parts of a flower.

69. Stem - Part of a plant that helps hold up the plant.

70. Tubes - The parts of plants that carry water and minerals from the soil to the leaves.

71. Wildflower - Flower that is not planted by people.

Frog life cycle

1. Frog spawn

2. Tadpole (Three weeks old)

3. Tadpole (Six weeks old)

4. Frog (Adult male)

Tadpole stage of life

1. Eggs -
2. Hatching
3. Free swimming
4. Teeth
5. Legs
6. Froglet

Hebrew Week Day Calendar

Names of the week day

Greek Hebrew

1.	Sunday	Yorn Rishon
2.	Monday	Yorn Sheni
3.	Tuesday	Yorn Shlishi
4.	Wednesday	Yorn Revi'i
5.	Thursday	Yorn Chamishi
6.	Friday	Yom Shishi
7.	Saturday	Yorn Shabbat

Hebrew Calendar

Hebrew Months

1.   Shevat - (January/February)

2.   Adar - (February/March)

3.   Nisan - {March/April)

4.   Iyyar - {April/May}

5.   Sivan - (May/June)

6.   Tammuz - {June/July)

7.   Av - {July/August)

8.   Elul - (August/September)

9.   Tishrei - (September/October)

10.   Heshvan - {October/November)

11.   Kislev - {November/December)

12.   Tevet - (December/January)

ABOUT THE BOOK

Alvin went through all kinds of challenges, trials, and tribulations. Nevertheless, he was kind and humble. Why? It was because of his mother. She used physical punishment on him, causing bodily harm. Later, someone came along and accepted him.